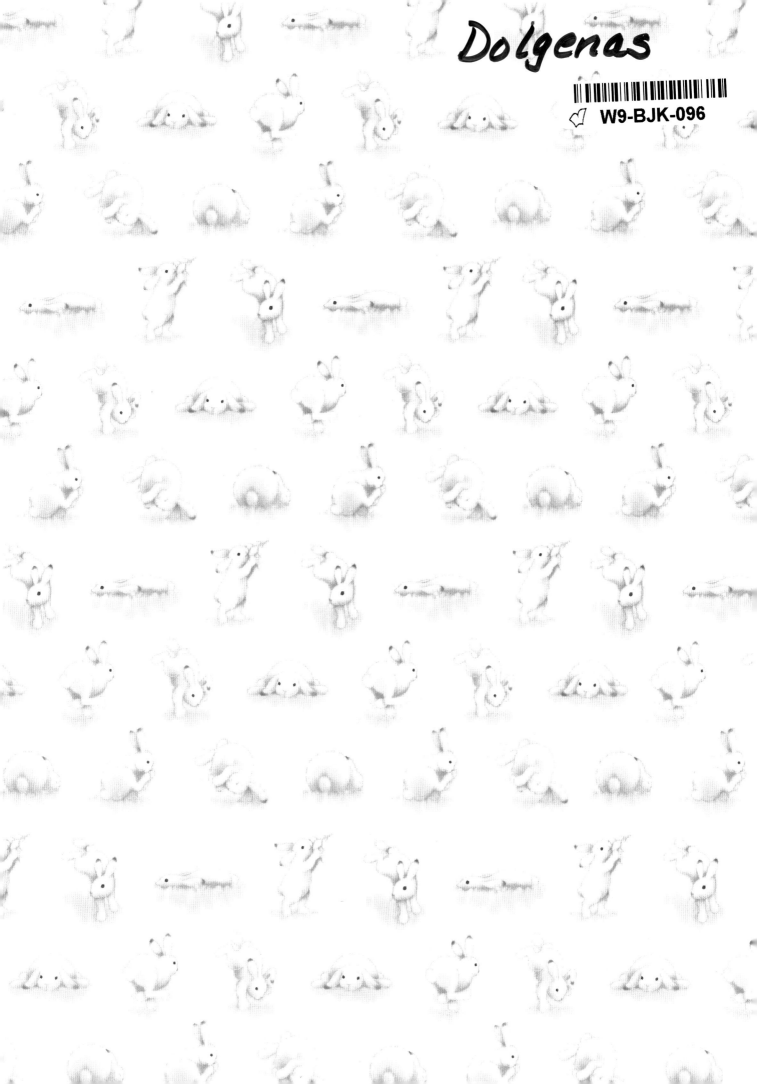

Dolgenas

For Miro Demian

Ask your bookseller for these other North-South books
illustrated by Marcus Pfister:

Four Candles for Simon, by Gerda Marie Scheidl
Miriam's Gift, by Gerda Marie Scheidl
Santa Claus and the Woodcutter, by Kathrin Siegenthaler

Books written and illustrated by Marcus Pfister:

Penguin Pete
Penguin Pete's New Friends
Penguin Pete and Pat
Where Is My Friend?
Sun and Moon
Shaggy

Copyright © 1991 by Nord-Süd Verlag AG, Gossau Zürich, Switzerland
First published in Switzerland under the title *Hoppel*
English translation copyright © 1991 by North-South Books, New York

First published in the United States, Great Britain, Canada,
Australia and New Zealand in 1991 by North-South Books,
an imprint of Nord-Süd Verlag AG, Gossau Zürich, Switzerland.

Library of Congress Cataloging-in-Publication Data
Pfister, Marcus.
[Hoppel. English]
Hopper/by Marcus Pfister.
Translation of: Hoppel.
Summary: Even though he doesn't like the cold snow, Hopper, a
little hare, enjoys playing with a friend and the adventure of
searching for food with his mother.
ISBN 1-55858-106-5
[1. Hares—Fiction. 2. Mother and child—Fiction.
3. Winter—Fiction.] I. Title.
PZ7.P448558Ho 1991
[E]—dc20   90-47065

British Library Cataloguing in Publication Data
Pfister, Marcus
Hopper.
I. Title II. [Hoppel, *English*]
833.914 [J]

ISBN 1-55858-106-5

1 3 5 7 9 10 8 6 4 2
Printed in Belgium

HOPPER

By Marcus Pfister

North-South Books / New York

"Wake up, Hopper!"

Mama gently pushed him with her nose. Hopper opened his eyes slowly and stretched himself.

"Do I have to wash myself again, Mama?"

"You ask the same question every day, Hopper. Don't you want your fur to stay white and healthy? Wash yourself and then you can play with your friend."

Hopper slowly licked his fur, starting with his paws.

He was a beautiful hare. His fur was pure white, like his mother's, but the tip of one of his ears was blue, which was very unusual.

When he had finished cleaning himself he ran over to Nick, who was still sleeping soundly under a bush.

Hopper tickled his nose and tapped his ears. But when Nick refused to wake up, Hopper just pulled him out from under the bush.

"What's going on?" muttered Nick sleepily. He tried to push Hopper away and soon the two started wrestling.

They made so much noise rolling around and laughing that the hedgehog woke up from hibernation. "Hey! Stop that noise!" he yelled. "I still have a month left to sleep."

"Sorry," said Nick softly. "We didn't realize you were there."

Wrestling in the snow had made Hopper hungry. "What is there to eat?" he asked his mother who was hopping by.

"Let's look for food together," said his mother.

"But I'd rather stay with Nick and play," Hopper said reluctantly. "Please bring me something."

"Come on now, don't be lazy," she said. "You can play with Nick tomorrow." So Hopper said goodbye to his friend and sullenly hopped away.

"Mama, wait! My paws are freezing. The snow is so cold."

"I know it's cold, but it's also white like we are so it's easier for us to hide from other animals."

"But why does it snow, Mama?"

"Most of the plants, bushes and grass have to rest in winter. When the snow melts in the spring it turns into water that helps them grow."

"Why do they need to rest?" asked Hopper, lying down in the snow. "They don't have to jump through the cold snow to look for food. I want to rest, too."

Suddenly Mama looked up and saw a falcon swooping down at them.

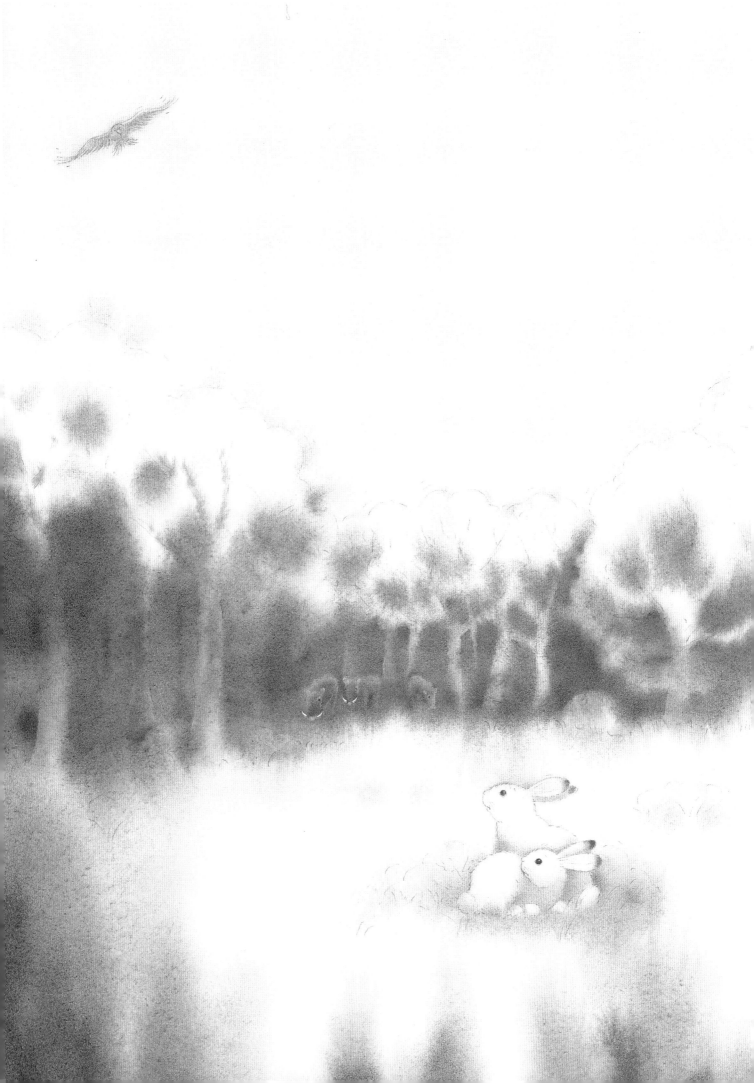

"Run!" she screamed. "Run as fast as you can to the forest and hide in the bushes!"

Hopper bounded away and his mother ran back and forth across the field to distract the falcon.

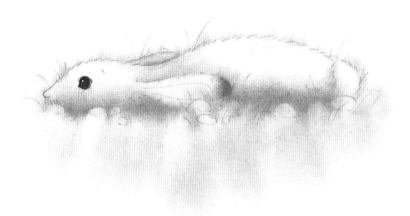

"Goodness, that was close," Mama sighed as the falcon flew away.

"What did that flying hare want?" asked Hopper.

"That was *not* a hare," she said sternly. "That was a falcon. I've warned you about falcons before. They love to grab little hares like you. That's why I've been trying to teach to you how to run back and forth across the open fields."

"But how could he see us? He was flying so high in the sky."

"Falcons have very strong eyes," his mother replied. "They're as dangerous as foxes. Come on, let's run back across the field."

Hopper tried to follow his mother, but when he turned too quickly he tumbled in the snow.

"Don't worry," said his mother. "You just need to keep trying. It wasn't easy for me to learn either."

Then the two of them went to look for food again.

Suddenly, Hopper came out of a bush, screaming, "Mama, a tree on four legs is after me."

His mother just laughed. "That's not a tree, that's a stag."

"A stag," Hopper repeated thoughtfully. "Will his branches grow leaves in the spring?"

"Those aren't branches," said his mother patiently. "Those are called antlers."

"And what does a stag need antlers for, Mama?"

"To defend himself against his enemies. And when he is hungry he uses them to dig in the ground to find food."

"I wish I had antlers," Hopper said quickly. "I'm starving."

"Here we are," said his mother. "This bark is very tasty."

"I don't like it," said Hopper, frowning. "It's so wet and cold. I'd rather eat some berries."

"There won't be berries until spring," she said, "so eat your bark like a good boy."

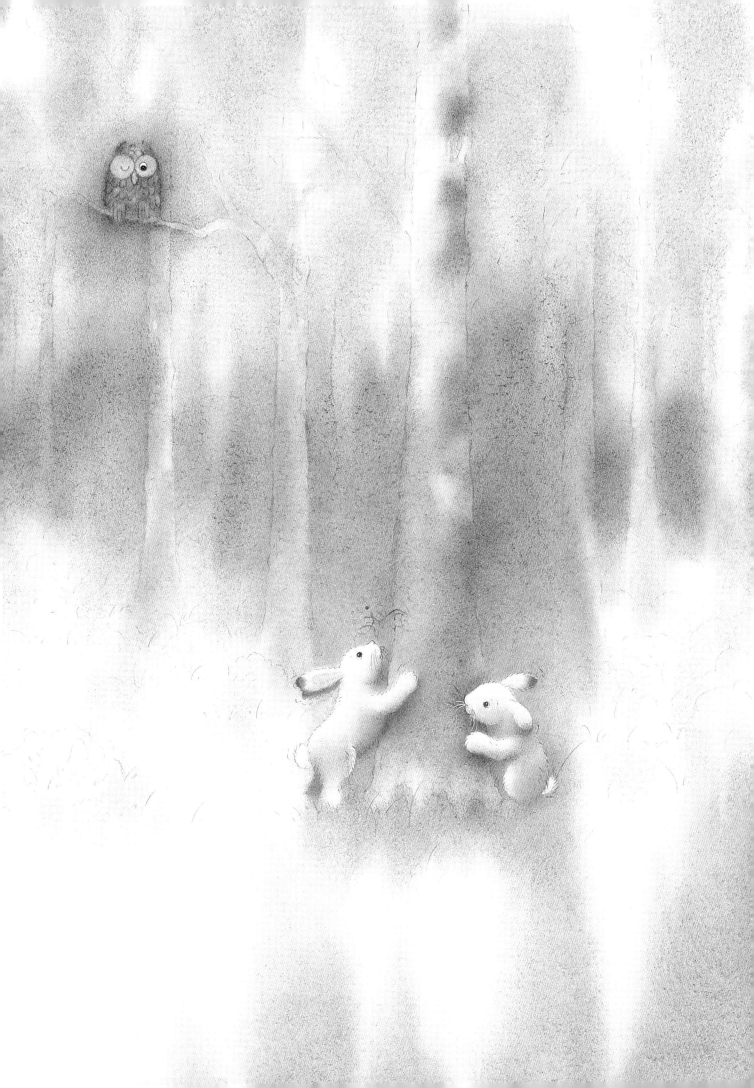

When the two of them were full they started to hop back home. The sun was going down and soon it would be dark.

"How far is it, Mama?" asked Hopper. "Will we be there soon? I'm tired."

"Don't worry, it's not far."

By the time they got home, the moon had come out and the stars were twinkling.

"Will the snow go away?" Hopper asked as he lay down.

"Yes," Mama said, as she gently stroked his back. "In spring, when the sun gets warmer, the snow will melt. Then the flowers will bloom in the fields and the leaves will grow on the trees. Farmers will plant their crops and we can search for carrots and lettuce. Would you like that?"

Hopper didn't say anything. He had already fallen asleep, dreaming of spring and juicy red berries.

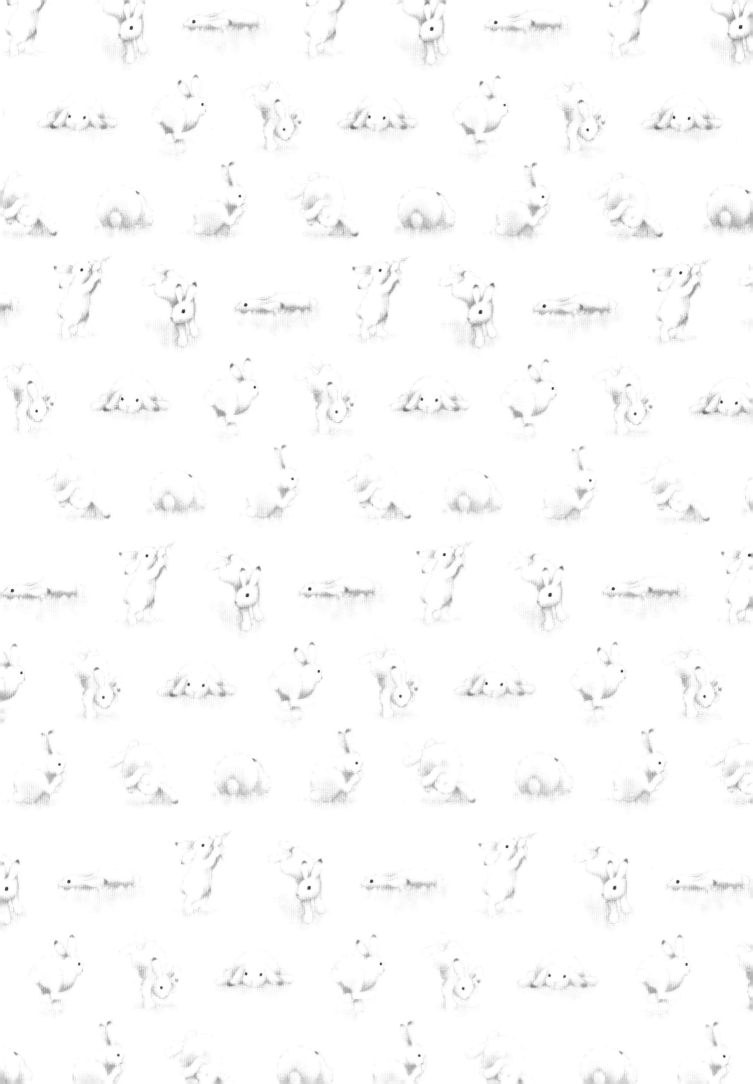